SLSN

D1148252

Wolf Goes to Sea

Llyfrgell S
dr

Powys

37218 00250001 0

To
Karen and Denis
at the Wellwisher Bookshop, Devizes

Published in Wales in 2008 by Pont Books, an imprint of
Gomer Press, Llandysul, Ceredigion, SA44 4JL

ISBN 978 1 84323 904 8
A CIP record for this title is available from the British Library.

© Copyright text and illustrations: Rob Lewis, 2008

The author / illustrator asserts his moral right under the
Copyright, Designs and Patents Act, 1988
to be identified as author and illustrator of this work.

All rights reserved. No part of this book may be reproduced,
stored in a retrieval system, or transmitted in any form
or by any means, electronic, electrostatic, magnetic tape, mechanical,
photocopying, recording or otherwise without permission
in writing from the above publishers.

This book is published with the financial support of the
Welsh Books Council.

Printed and bound in Wales at
Gomer Press, Llandysul, Ceredigion

Wolf Goes to Sea

Rob Lewis

Pont

In a small harbour town as cosy can be
lived the last wolf in Wales in a house by the sea.
Nain, his best friend, owned the teashop next door
where he liked to sip tea and look out on the shore.

But often he sat on the old harbour wall,
looking lonely and gloomy – not happy at all.
Nain finally said, 'What's the matter with you?
I don't like to see you so sad and so blue.'
'Nain, you're my friend but I hope you don't mind –
I just need some closeness with those of my kind,'
said the wolf as his eyes wandered over the sea.
'Out there somewhere waiting are wolves just like me.'

'I would help you,' said Nain, 'but I haven't much money.
Where do wolves live? Is it somewhere quite sunny?'
'They live in the north where the sunlight is dim
and where pine forests grow and the weather is grim.
And how I will get there I really don't know.
It seems an incredibly long way to go.'
'If you're eager,' said Nain, 'to set off on this trip,
you will need to find somewhere to hide on a ship.'

Then as they watched at the end of the day,
they spied a large vessel right out in the bay.

So Nain rowed them out to the ship in the night
and the wolf sneaked aboard before it got light.

He found a container – he thought it would suit –
it was stacked high with dog food and tropical fruit.

There's plenty of space and plenty to eat,
thought the wolf, looking round. This place is a treat!
Then he found some old sacks and he made up a bed
and closed the lid tightly right over his head.
With torches for light it looked very cosy
and after a while the wolf felt quite dozy.

He fell fast asleep to the ship engine sound
'til he woke up to find all his food thrown around.
Outside it was windy with mountainous seas
and he started to quiver and quake at the knees.

To stop getting wet,
he shut the lid quick
and sank in the corner
– he felt rather sick!

At last, the wolf slept through
the noise of the sea

and when he awoke it was calm as could be.
He opened the lid. But where was the boat?
At least his container was staying afloat.

The box drifted north for more than a week.
It rained and it snowed   the weather was bleak.
The blizzards and hailstorms were really not nice
but worse was to come when the box struck some ice.

Marooned on an iceberg, with no one in view,
the wolf felt so lonely but what could he do?
A seagull dropped in but he only spoke 'gull'
so the wolf sat in silence – which made the days dull.

Then one day he heard the ground rumble and shake.
The ice that was under him started to break.
The iceberg had stuck in a small rocky bay
but where in the world, he just could not say.

Carefully stepping, he made for the shore
and wondered what dangers there might be in store.

A blizzard was blowing. He started to freeze
so he looked for some shelter among the fir trees.
Deep in the forest he got a surprise.
Out of the darkness came four pairs of eyes.

They were wolves just like him! He had found them at last.
He forgot all the trouble he'd had in the past.
'Welcome to Finland,' they said with delight.
'Wolves from abroad are a very rare sight!'
They showed him the way as fast as they could
to their secret wolf den in the heart of the wood.
They asked him about all the sights he had seen
and all of the marvellous places he'd been.

He looked at them sadly and said with dismay,
'I saw only water and snow every day.
I travelled by sea and not on the land
and things didn't quite go the way I had planned.'
Then he sat by the fire, enjoying the heat,
and told them his tale as he toasted his feet.
'We could see things were bad by the state you were in.
But now that we've found you, the fun can begin!'

The wolves threw a party. It went on and on
'til the wolf's thoughts of home had almost all gone.
But then he remembered poor Nain on her own.
He shouldn't have left her so long all alone.
The wolves here were great but he had to admit:
the cold and the dark he did not like one bit.

'Sorry,' he said, 'but I think I must go.
I have friends back in Wales who'll miss me you know.
But after my shipwreck, I don't think I'll sail.'
'In that case,' they said, 'you must travel by rail.'

They found him a train and he said his goodbyes.
All of his friends had tears in their eyes.
They helped him aboard and they wished him good luck.
Then he sat and he waved from the top of his truck.

He travelled to Russia and passed by Red Square
but slept all through Poland so saw nothing there.

Then he watched German forests and castles go by,
with towers and walls that reached up to the sky.

In Holland he saw lots of people on bikes
and fields full of tulips and windmills and dykes.

The train stopped in Paris – he managed a glance
at the tall Eiffel Tower, the most famous in France.

Then travelling on, he went under the sea
then homeward to Wales where he wanted to be.

Nain gave him a hug as she welcomed him in.
'I'm glad you're back safely,' she said with a grin.
'But leaving your friends must have been really hard
so why don't you sit down and write them a card?'

'I'll write to them now,' said the wolf. 'Then, you'll see, some day in the future, they'll all visit me.'

The Wolves

Den in the Forest

North Finland

EUROPE

Why don't you write a letter to the wolves in the north?
Tell them about where you live or a place you have visited
on holiday.